Where Do People Go When They Die?

Mindy Avra Portnoy   illustrations by Shelly O. Haas

KAR-BEN
PUBLISHING

For my mother, Sarah Themper Portnoy,
and my Rabbi, Andrew Klein. They make my
heart strong, as I remember them always.
M.A.P.

For my grandmother and for all those
in whose hearts she lives on.
S.O.H.

KAR-BEN PUBLISHING
A division of Lerner Publishing Group, Inc.
241 First Avenue North
Minneapolis, MN 55401 U.S.A.
1-800-4KARBEN

Website address: www.karben.com

Library of Congress Cataloging-in-Publication Data

Portnoy, Mindy Avra.
  Where do people go when they die? / by Mindy Portnoy ; illustrated by Shelly O. Haas.
    p. cm.
Summary: Children ask different adults and themselves about death and receive a wide variety of answers.
Includes an afterword and suggestions for parents.
  ISBN-13: 978-1-58013-081-3 (lib. bdg. : alk. paper)
  ISBN-10: 1-58013-081-X (lib. bdg. : alk. paper)
  [1. Death—Fiction. 2. Questions and answers—Fiction.] I. Haas, Shelly O., ill. II. Title.
  PZ7.P8375 Wh 2003
  [E]—dc21
                          2002151694

Manufactured in the United States of America
4 5 6 7 8 9 — JR — 13 12 11 10 09 08

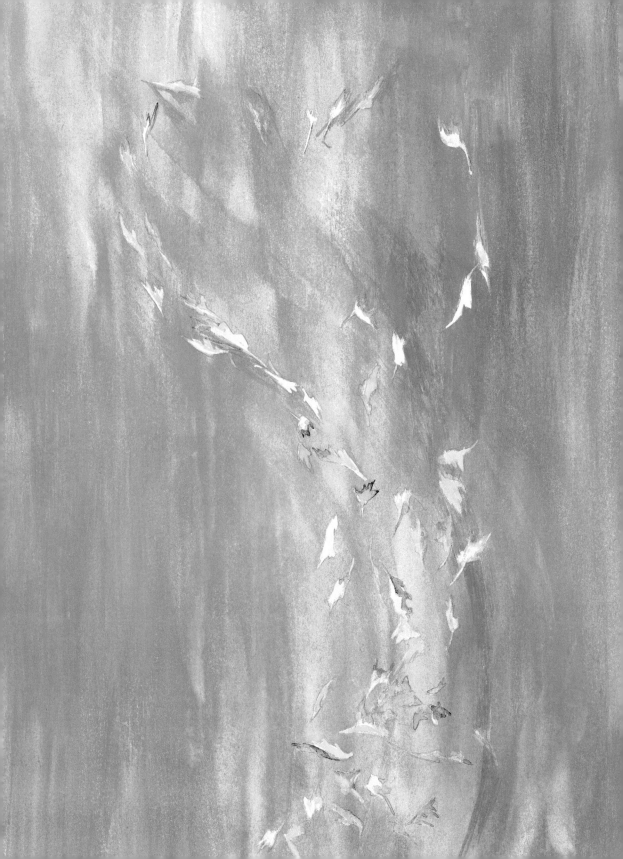

"Where do people go when they die?"
I asked my father.

"They are buried in the ground,"
he said, "and become part of
the earth and of nature."

"Where do people go when they die?" I asked my mother.

"They go to heaven, a place
of peace," she answered.

"They watch over us from there."

"Where do people
go when they die?"
I asked my
grandfather.

"They go into our memories and our stories about them. They become part of our minds," he said.

"They become the past."

"Where do people go when they die?" I asked my aunt.

"They go into our hearts," she said.

"They are with us when
we cry and when we
laugh. They are with us
as we grow up and grow
old. They make our
hearts strong," she said.

"Where do people go when they die?"
I asked my teacher.

"They live on in their children, their
students, their friends...in all the people
whom they loved and cared about.

They become the future."

"Where do people go when they die?"
I asked myself.

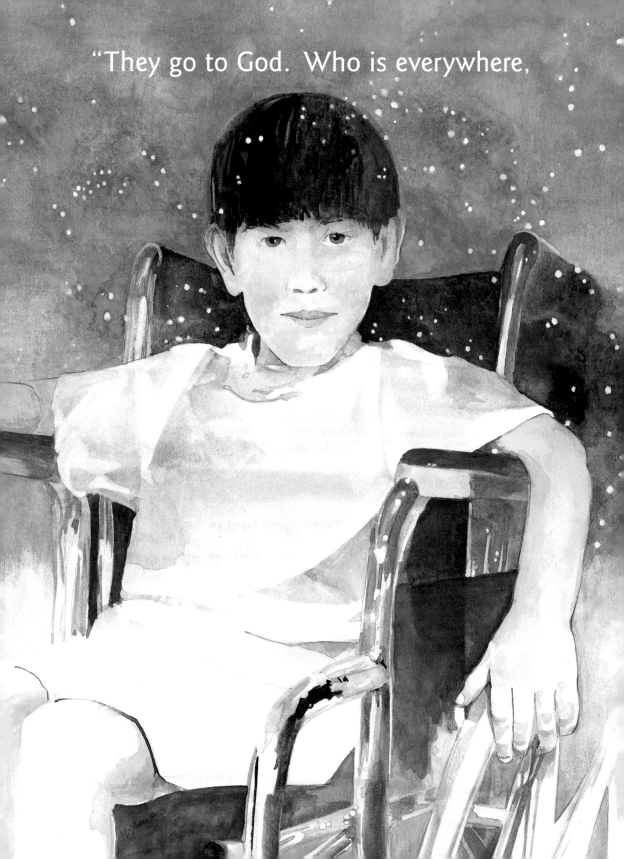

"They go to God. Who is everywhere,

In heaven and on earth,
In our minds and in our hearts,
In the past and in the future,

In each of us who
remembers them
always."

Afterword

Every child asks about death sooner or later. Sometimes the questions arise because of the death of a pet, a grandparent's death, or, most tragically, the death of a parent, sibling, or young friend. Other times a child is motivated to ask the question by a news report on television, a movie, or an overheard discussion.

Whenever the question occurs, many parents are at a loss for words. "What are the right answers?" they ask themselves. "Which may damage my child psychologically — honesty or 'white lies?' What do I personally believe about death and related topics such as an 'afterlife?'"

As a rabbi, I hear these questions often. I respond that like most answers to profound philosophical questions, there is no "right" or "wrong" answer. But there ARE "better" or "worse" approaches to the subject. The better approaches couple honesty with gentleness, openness with support. Better answers are age and developmentally appropriate, and they respond to the question the child is really asking.

Some examples:

What happened to Grandpa?
"Grandpa died. He is not sleeping or away on a trip. 'Dying' means Grandpa is not coming back."

Your child needs to know the truth, and you need to support that truth with the facts.

"Grandpa was very old and sick. We will miss him very much. We can look at pictures and tell stories about Grandpa to help us remember him."

It will be somewhat easier for children to understand Grandpa's dying if you have kept them informed about Grandpa's health beforehand. Sometimes we try so hard to "protect" our children, that it is actually more difficult for them when death occurs.

When a death is sudden or unexpected, parents need to admit that such deaths do happen, but not often.

Will you die, too?
"Yes, but not for a long time."

Most children worry about losing their parents, once they understand the reality of death. A parent's job is to bolster their child's sense of security, without denying the truth.

Will I die, too?
"Yes, death is a part of every life, but usually people die when they're old."

Children learn soon enough that fatal illnesses and accidents can happen even to young people, but you should answer the question by talking first about what is most likely.

Suggestions for Parents

1. Do not answer more than your child has asked, or more than he/she is ready to absorb. In this sense, it is like talking about sex.

2. Be honest. Say "some people believe this" and "some people believe that" if there are questions you are not certain about. Don't pretend to believe in something in which you do not believe (heaven, or an afterlife, for example), but leave options open for your children.

3. Use books, movies, and television shows to help in your conversation. A librarian, teacher, or clergy person can help you choose age-appropriate material.

4. Call on others if you need them as resources, but consider yourself the principal teacher/mentor to your child. You shouldn't ALWAYS have to say, "We'll go ask the rabbi or minister."

5. Prepare your child for what will happen at the funeral or memorial service, and at the cemetery. Lack of information is more frightening than knowledge. If you are not certain, ask the officiating clergy or a friend to explain.

6. Help your child create a memory book about the person, including pictures and words.

7. Do not be surprised if your child asks "unusual" questions. At his grandfather's funeral, my five-year-old son asked, "Won't his clothes get dirty in the ground?" A little boy who's worried about keeping his clothes clean would see that as a normal question. Other children may ask what will happen to the deceased person's possessions. Share this information with your child.

8. Do not be dismayed if your child does NOT ask a lot of questions, but also do not mistake silence for lack of concern. Children, like adults, grieve in different ways. Be alert for changes in behavior.

9. If a child becomes obsessed with death or has continuing nightmares, seek professional help from a counseling service or clergy.

Mindy Avra Portnoy is the author of three previous books, including *Matzah Ball: A Passover Story*. Rabbi Portnoy is a graduate of Yale University, and was ordained at Hebrew Union College-Jewish Institute of Religion. She is a rabbi in Washington, D.C., is married and has two children.

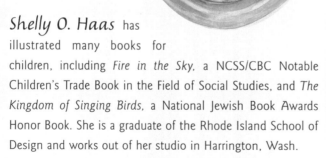

Shelly O. Haas has illustrated many books for children, including *Fire in the Sky*, a NCSS/CBC Notable Children's Trade Book in the Field of Social Studies, and *The Kingdom of Singing Birds*, a National Jewish Book Awards Honor Book. She is a graduate of the Rhode Island School of Design and works out of her studio in Harrington, Wash.